Chelsea
and Cham

Written by Mary Hooper
Illustrated by Lucy Su

Hooked On Phonics®

Hooked On Phonics®

This version © 1998 Gateway Learning Corporation. The original work entitled, *Gita and Goldie*
Text Copyright © by Mary Hooper 1998. Illustrations Copyright © by Lucy Su 1998. Published by Bloomsbury Publishing Plc.
ISBN 1-887942-64-5   6 7 8 9 10

Contents

1. Let Champ Decide

"Champ's basket is going to be
in *my* room," Patty said.

"No, it's going to be in *mine*!"
said Chelsea.

The two girls stood, one on each
side of Champ.

Champ did not know what they were talking about, but he knew they were talking about him. He panted happily. He liked them talking about him.

"I can have him because my room's bigger," Patty said.

"But mine's much nicer," said Chelsea. "He'd rather be in my room."

"Oh, no, he would not!"

"Yes, he would!"

It was moving day. Patty, Chelsea, their mom and dad, and Champ were moving from a small house in town to a bigger house in the suburbs.

The family had just arrived at
the new house in their car. Now
they were all waiting for the
moving van to get there.

As soon as they arrived, Patty and Chelsea ran upstairs to see which bedroom they wanted. Patty could pick first because she was the oldest.

She picked the bigger one. Chelsea
was left with smaller one. She had
to pretend that *her* bedroom was
much nicer.

Now they were fighting
about Champ. In their old house,
they had shared a bedroom.
Champ's basket had been between
their beds.

Chelsea looked out of the
window. "Here's the moving van
coming down the road!"

"I tell you what," Patty said. "When we have moved into our rooms, we can let Champ decide where he wants to be."

"All right," Chelsea said, but she was not happy. Patty was older than Chelsea, so she always got to do more things with Champ. He was more used to her. He might like to be in her room better!

"May the best girl win!" Patty said, and she bent over and gave Champ a pat.

"Yes...," said Chelsea, but she was not so sure. She gave Champ a pat too.

"Woof!" said Champ. He loved being the center of attention!

2. What a Mess!

"I'm going to get Champ's
basket out of the van," Patty said.

"No, you are not!" Chelsea said.
"I'm getting it!"

The two girls ran to the door.
Their mom was coming in with
a big stack
of books.

They ran smack into her, and the
books scattered all over the hall.
    "Patty! Chelsea!" their mom
said. "For goodness' sake!"

"Sorry, Mom." The girls bent down to pick up the books.

"There's lots to do. Why can't you two do something useful besides racing around the house?"

"We were!" Patty said.

"We were getting Champ's basket out of the van," Chelsea said.

Their mom said, "We can't reach his basket until we have unpacked everything."

"Oh," they sighed.

"So you two can go into the kitchen and unpack the plates."

"Can I take Champ for a run?" Patty asked. "It would get him out from under your feet."

"That's just what I was going to do!" Chelsea said.

21

"I want you two in the kitchen!" their mom said. "Now!"

They unpacked a big pile of plates, cups, saucers, and bowls that had been wrapped in newspaper. As they unwrapped, they tossed the paper in back of them.

   By the time they had finished,
there was a very big pile of
newspaper.
   Champ came in and ran into
the pile. He jumped and barked.
He scattered the newspaper all
over the kitchen. The two girls
giggled happily.

Then their mom came in.
"What is going on?" she said.
"That silly dog! And you two are not helping!"
"Sorry, Mom," Patty said quickly.

"We'll pick it all up," said Chelsea.

Mom sighed. "When you are finished, you can go up to your rooms and start unpacking your boxes."

Patty nodded. She looked down at Champ, who was panting.

"Let's go make my room all nice, OK, Champ? Then you can pick which corner you want your basket in."

Chelsea let out a cry. "Mom! Champ is not sleeping in *her* room, is he?"

"Oh, goodness!" their mom said. "I have better things to think about than a dog's bed. Now get to work."

Chelsea and Patty started picking up the newspaper, each thinking of a "get Champ" plan.

3. Champ Picks

It was late afternoon. The girls
had set up their new rooms. Their
clothes were hung up. Their books
were unpacked. Everything that
could be set up without the help of
a grown-up was set up.

While they were working, they had been trying to get Champ into their bedrooms.

Chelsea had gone downstairs and found Champ's box of dog treats.

Then she made a little trail of
them up the stairs, down the hall,
and into her room. Champ had
eaten his way up and right to her.

When Patty found out, she went right into the kitchen and got a can of Champ's dog food. She opened it and put it under her bed.

Soon Champ smelled it. He came running out of Chelsea's room and right into Patty's room.

At three o'clock, Champ's basket came out of the van.

"Will you put it in my room, please?" Patty said to the man as he carried it in.

"No, in mine!" Chelsea said.

The girls' dad came in.

"Where do you want it, mister?" the man asked him.

"Just put it upstairs, please," their dad said. "The girls can work it out later."

First Patty took the basket into her room.

And then Chelsea ran in and
snatched it back.

Then their mom came up. "Go
to your rooms. I do not want to
hear one more peep out of you,"
she said. "And Champ stays
out in the hall."

After a little while, Patty knocked on Chelsea's door.

"Let's have Champ pick now," she said. "You go in your room, and I will go in mine, and we will each call him. The one he goes to can have his basket in her room."

Chelsea stopped for a bit. Then she said, "OK."

The girls each patted Champ and said, "Stay!"

Then they went into their rooms
and shouted for him.

"Here, boy!" Patty called.

"Come on, Champ!"
Chelsea called.

"Good dog!" called Patty.

"Here, Champ!" said Chelsea.

Champ looked from one to the other. Then he ran into Patty's room, wagging his tail.

He ran right up to Patty, who made a big fuss over him.

"See?" she said. "Champ stays with me because he loves me the best!"

"No, he does not!" Chelsea said. "He does not!"

Then she ran downstairs and out into the garden.

4. Chelsea Is Sad

Chelsea kicked at a tree. She was so mad! Why did Champ pick Patty over her?

Chelsea went right down to the bottom of the garden where no one could see her. She knew she was going to hate living here.

Champ loved Patty better than her!

She kicked at the fence. There were two planks missing. She could see down the road.

What if . . . what if she crawled through and went for a walk? She could look around a bit, and she could also see if anyone missed her.

She did not remember all the times her mom had said never to go off by herself. She just went through and began walking down the road.

"They will see," she said to herself. "If I do not come back for a while, maybe they will all be nice to me."

Before she knew it, she was at the end of the road. The road turned from a paved road into a dirt track that curved into the woods.

   There were big trees deeper in,
but at the side there was just a
grassy patch with green and
yellow bushes. It looked very
pretty.
   Two squirrels ran off down the
path, and Chelsea ran after them
into the woods. She was enjoying
the walk. She hoped they would
miss her at home.

As she walked, she looked back at the bright yellow bushes. But the path had curved around too much for her to see them.

She saw a rabbit and went off the path to the right. Then she saw some wildflowers and went off to the left.

Soon the woods got darker. All she could see was trees...more and more trees. It was getting darker and darker.

She remembered her mom and dad telling her *never* to go out without letting someone know where she was going...never to go off by herself.

But she remembered all these things too late. Because she was lost.

5. Champ, the Champ

Back at the house, everyone knew Chelsea was not there, and everyone was upset.

"I did not know she would go off!" Patty said.

"Did you two have a fight?" Mom asked.

"Not really," Patty said, feeling badly.

The moving men had left.
Everyone had looked all over
the house for Chelsea. They
looked in the shed and the garden.
   That's when they saw that there
were two planks missing from the
fence at the end of the garden.

"I think she went through the fence," Dad said.

"She would not do that!" said Mom. "I have said over and over…" She broke off and started crying.

"It's getting dark now," Patty said. She felt like crying too.

"Call the police!" Mom said.

"But we do not have a phone yet!" Dad said. He patted his pockets for his car keys. "I will go into town. I will get the police to come out."

Mom wiped her tears. "I will stay here and look some more."

"I will go with Dad," sniffed Patty.

Patty and her dad went out to the car. Champ went with them. He was quiet and sad.

Dad said, "I will stop at a store and ask where the police station is." He turned the car and drove away from the woods, into the town.

As they drove off, Champ jumped to the back seat and started barking.

"Hush!" Dad yelled.

Champ went on barking.

"Can't you make him stop?" Dad asked Patty.

"Quiet, Champ!" Patty said. "Can't you see we are upset? Chelsea is lost."

When Patty said "Chelsea,"
Champ gave a short, sharp yelp.
He pricked up his ears. He tilted
his head to one side.

"Dad!" Patty said. "I think
Champ is trying to tell us
something."

"Don't be silly," Dad said. "Now, should I go right or left here…?"

Champ began barking again, looking out the back window.

"Dad!" Patty said again. "I know… I think…he seems to…"

Champ barked over and over again. Then he began to whine, scratching at the back door of the car.

56

"Could we just turn back?" Patty asked. "I think Champ knows where Chelsea is."

"We can't stop now!" Dad said. "It's getting darker."

"*Please*, Dad!" Patty pleaded.

So Dad turned the car around. Champ stopped barking right away.

Dad drove back the way they had come. Every now and then Champ would give a short, sharp bark. It was as if he was saying, "Yes, this is right...."

They drove past their new house and down the road to where it ended in a dirt track. Dad stopped the car. Champ put his paws on the window.

He looked down the path Chelsea had taken and panted hard.

Dad let him out of the car, and Champ looked around as if to say, "Come with me!" Then he ran.

He led them down the path.
He went deeper and deeper into
the woods. Patty and her dad had
to run to keep up.

"How could he know where to go?"
Dad said.

"Don't ask me!" Patty gasped.

It was so dark that, as they ran,
they tripped over fallen branches.
At last they came to a clearing
with one big tree in the center.
Standing under the tree, crying
softly, was Chelsea.

● ● ●

Back at the house, Chelsea
had been checked and hugged by
everyone. Her mom and dad said,
"Please do not do that again!"

"I just do not understand it," Dad said. "That dog ran right to her!"

Chelsea smiled and hugged Champ.

"He came to find me. Maybe he loves me just as much as Patty after all!"

Patty put her arm around Chelsea. "I know he does," she said. "Let's have him sleep in my room one week, and yours the next."

"Woof!" said Champ. He'd done something really special, and he knew it. Now he'd be the center of attention forever!